WARM-UPS FOR CHANGING VOICES
Building Healthy Middle School Singers

BY DAN ANDERSEN

HAL•LEONARD®
7777 W. BLUEMOUND RD. P.O. BOX 13819 MILWAUKEE, WI 53213

ISBN-13: 978-1-49508-798-1
ISBN-10: 1-49508-798-0

Published by Hal Leonard Corporation
7777 W. Bluemound Road
P.O. Box 13819
Milwaukee, WI 53213

Visit Hal Leonard Online at
www.halleonard.com

In Australia contact:
Hal Leonard Australia Pty. Ltd.
4 Lentara Court
Cheltenham, Victoria, 3192 Australia

Email: ausadmin@halleonard.com.au

7777 W. BLUEMOUND RD. P.O. BOX 13819 MILWAUKEE, WI 53213

Contents

Dedication

This book is dedicated to my dad, Daniel Paul Andersen. I could not have asked for a better role model. He made everyone he came in contact with feel better about themselves. He was the most positive, patient, and loving person I've ever known. Thank you, dad, for showing me how to be a better husband, father, person, and teacher. I love you and miss you!

 # Acknowledgments

First and foremost, I would like to thank my wife Kim; my four children Erica, Stacie, Chelsea, and Daniel; as well as their spouses Josh, Brandon, Caleb, and Kailyn; for their support. They have been a big part of this 35-year journey, and many of them have even sung in a choir or two of mine over the years!

I would like to thank my mom Theresa, and my siblings Cindy, Tim, John, Dave, and Tom, for their encouragement and ability to keep me humble!

I would like to thank Dave and Kristie Kaufman for their constant support. Dave not only gave me the idea to write a book, but has also been a great sounding board along the way.

I would like to thank some of my more influential music teachers, including John Loessi, Joe and Violette Meyers, Bill Schlacks, and Dave Streeter. Most of all, I want to thank Fr. Fred Link, my high school choir director. He showed me how to love one's students and push them toward excellence. He also sparked in me a love of choral singing, and he "nudged" me toward a career in music education.

A special thanks goes to my good friend and mentor Jane Brewer. I had the pleasure of working alongside her when I made the switch back to middle school after 14 years of teaching high school. I learned so much from her; I believe I am the teacher I am today because of Jane.

I would like to thank Alisa Isaacs and Jack Haggenjos for their help along the way with some editing.

Finally, I would especially like to thank the countless students who have passed through my classroom and into my heart. I do what I do for you. I push myself to learn as much as I can so you can be the best that you can be. You have made me a better teacher and, more importantly, a better person. Thank you for the "handprint on my heart!"

Introduction

I have had the opportunity to work with adolescent voices for more than 35 years as a private voice instructor and choral director. Developing the young voice into a mature adult voice, in a healthy way, has become a passion for me. I've found that through a well-developed set of warm-ups, applied systematically to a choir, you can develop healthy voices and healthy singing habits. You can also keep your students more interested and less frustrated, encouraging them to stay involved in choir through high school and into adulthood.

We have all found warm-ups that either work or don't work for our choirs. And we've also found great warm-ups that work for some choirs, but not others. I hope to show you how to tailor your warm-ups to each grade-level singer in middle school. I will discuss some possible mistakes that are made and give you tips to help avoid them. I will provide a collection of warm-ups that I have used successfully over the years and show you how I apply each of them across the grades. My hope is that you will find some ideas to help bring new life and purpose into your choral rehearsal.

So, why warm up? I think we all remember back to our own voice lessons, and that's just what we did before we worked on literature. The same went for piano lessons. How many scales did we do before we walked into that studio for our lesson? Did we ever think to ask why? As you know, that's what middle school students do best! I had to have a strong rationale as to why we were spending time every day "not singing songs!" I've found that if you have good reasons for middle school students to do something, they will give it their all. But if you don't, you may have some behavior issues on your hands!

As a middle school teacher, I use a lot of analogies in my teaching. I try to learn what's "in" for the kids, and to make connections that make sense to them. I tend to use a lot of sports analogies because many of my students are involved in travel athletics and competitive dance, and they understand the connections I'm trying to make. For example, I tell them frequently that choir is the ultimate team sport. By this I mean that every single member of our team is a starter; there are no subs! If someone is singing

a wrong note, I can't call for a sub from the bench. I also tell them that every one of them is the point guard. (Since I teach in Indiana, basketball references are common! For those of you who didn't grow up playing basketball, almost every play runs through the point guard. That position is an extremely important part of a successful team. It is the equivalent of a quarterback in football.) One of the most obvious connections I make for them is between excellent singing posture and an athletic stance. I will demonstrate for them how professionals like Peyton Manning, Derek Jeter, and Kerri Walsh Jennings would stand, and why. From there it's much easier to get them to buy into excellent singing posture. These athletic analogies have paid big dividends for me over the years!

So when I tell students that **conditioning** is one of the reasons we warm-up, they get it. Singing is a physical activity, and I expect them to involve their whole body, just as an athlete does. Conditioning is starting earlier and earlier all the time with our young athletes. Whether or not we agree with it, many kids are lifting weights, doing agility training, or involved in other similar activities as early as 1st grade. They know that when they run every day, or do ten reps of ten curls every workout, or whatever conditioning they're doing, they are going to see results. If we can get them to view our daily warm-ups in the same way, we will get them to hear the results in their voice that we are after.

Athletes typically **stretch** before they practice, or right before a game or meet. They do this to prevent pulling muscles, and to ensure their bodies are ready to perform their best no matter what comes their way. My choirs do a physical stretch before we even start to vocalize. Then we stretch our voices before we sing so we are ready for whatever vocal challenges we may encounter in the music.

Building our voices is another reason we warm-up. Like athletes, who are always working toward "bigger, faster, stronger," we are striving for similar results. Our students need the ability to sing louder with control and accuracy, to maneuver quick passages with control and consistency, and to produce a more intense tone no matter the dynamic level.

Developing an excellent **tone quality** is another important reason for our warm-ups. Just as the golfer focuses on developing the technique behind the "perfect swing," we try to do the same with our tone quality. There is a lot to be said for muscle memory. If you do something enough times, it will happen without thinking. This is where I tell them that practice doesn't make perfect—it makes permanent! *Perfect practice* makes perfect. We can focus on developing a beautiful tone more easily during warm-ups than while working in literature. This makes it easier to apply a beautiful tone to the literature!

Other important benefits of warming up are developing excellent **breath control** and proper **breathing technique**. It is more efficient to isolate the breathing process through exercises than to teach it in the midst of working on literature. We are also isolating **specific areas of growth**, or **difficult areas** for our singers. For example, our young men need daily work on developing their head voices and minimizing their "breaks." In fact, all singers need help in their *passagios* (register breaks or passage areas), especially the young singer. If the choir is performing a piece that has quick passages, we will want to address that in our warm-ups. If the choir is singing an a cappella piece, we would want to focus on choral warm-ups that stress intonation.

Conditioning, stretching, building voices, developing better tone quality, improving breathing technique/breath support, and isolating specific areas of growth are the main reasons we have our students vocalize daily. It's important to realize that you are the only voice teacher that 95% of your students will ever have. I approach every class like it's a voice lesson for my students. As a choir director, I am responsible for their vocal growth and their vocal health. It is my responsibility to know the voice in general, and know *their* voices specifically. If you have  never taken a vocal pedagogy course, take one now. *You* have to know how to build a healthy voice. *You* have to know where the trouble areas are for your 6th grade girls, 7th grade boys, and all the rest of your students. *You* have to become the expert so they can learn and grow.

A little knowledge goes a long way, but a lot of knowledge will give your students a foundation of healthy, beautiful singing for a lifetime!

Section 1
Gender and Grade

At first, I wasn't quite sure what to call this chapter. I thought about "Boys vs. Girls," but that sounds like they're going to battle (even though it seems like they are at times!). My real focus here is to discuss vocal issues that are typical of each gender at each grade level, and what voice parts I have my students sing. I want to get the most out of them, but I also want to make sure they are comfortable vocally.

Most of these observations are general. They are based on 35 years of working with the adolescent voice, both in the classroom and in the private studio. And, everything I say has an exception. You may say, "Well sure, but what about Jimmy? He sings a (fill-in-the-blank pitch). What do I do with him?" That's a very good question! Let's stick with the general for now, and see if we can get to the "exceptional" students in the process.

Grade 6 (in General)

6th grade boys and girls, "vocally" speaking, can be treated the same. My goal for all of them is to get them to sing, and be comfortable, using their head voices. Most of the singing we do is in the treble clef, both in warm-ups and literature. (Using quality literature is another very important key to developing beautiful, healthy voices. It's also a key to classroom management. But that's a whole different book!) Developing a strong head voice is imperative to developing a strong adult male voice. Laying that foundation in the 6th grade will pay big dividends later on.

Our young ladies need this same foundation on which to build. A focused, intense head voice will do much more for them than a big chest voice with nothing above it. This isn't to say that we ignore the lower range, but we should spend more time developing and singing in their head voices. Understandably, many of the girls come in wanting to sing like their favorite pop star. I don't poo-poo this. (I'm a big fan of Lady Gaga!) Most voice teachers who teach the "belt" style will tell you that they build it from the top down, not the bottom up. There has to be a strong, healthy head voice upon which to build that blended belt voice. Listen to Kristin Chenoweth and you can hear both a gorgeous head voice and a powerful, blended belt voice.

Let's talk specific genders now. Ladies first!

Girls (in General)

The amount of information available on the changing male voice is staggering! Google it sometime. Not only are there books and articles, but there are chapters in every choral music textbook dealing, in great depth, with the male changing voice. Conversely, there is very little written on the female changing voice. I think we are at the start of a new wave of information on the changing female voice, however—which I think is about 30-40 years late in coming.

My intent here is not to go into great detail about the changing voice. I encourage you to do that research and become the expert in your classroom for your students. My goal is to discuss the areas in which they struggle, based on my research and experiences, and provide ideas to help them. So here we go!

Middle school girls, generally speaking, struggle with intensity, strength, range, volume, and their passagios. These are the areas we need to develop. The process of developing the young female voice is a slow process. I've had girls who developed all of these areas very quickly and sang with a focused, mature sound as an 8th grader. I've also had those who, even after years of private voice lessons, still struggled with one or more of these areas as an 18-year old! My own daughters are great examples of this. Chelsea had a lovely, natural vibrato by 8th grade, while Erica's didn't develop until her junior year of high school. Stacie had a powerhouse voice (from birth!) and didn't have to focus on her breath support as much. Erica worked and worked on breath support, but never developed the power of the other two. Erica did develop a stunning, lyric soprano voice, and was a late bloomer vocally, like her father.

Very few young ladies are true sopranos or altos in middle school. My philosophy is to have them all sing both parts at some point during their time with me. My own daughters did this when they sang in my choirs, and they have developed vocal flexibility, as well as the ability to blend.

Grade 6 Girls

Over the years, the biggest issue I've noticed with my in-coming 6th graders is an inability to access their head voices with consistency. This is one of my main areas of focus for my 6th grade girls. I want them to be able to readily access their head voice, and do so comfortably. This is often a major adjustment, as most of their vocal models sing only in their chest voice, and usually somewhat in their throat.

In my choirs, at the beginning of the 6th grade, all of the girls will sing in the same section. For half of the songs, they will sing part I (soprano) and the boys will sing part II (alto). Then they switch parts for the other songs. In addition to developing their upper range by singing soprano, they also get the experience of singing a harmony part by singing alto. Not only are you developing strong, healthy voices, but you are developing strong musicians as well.

After our first concert, we do another voice chart. Using that information, I assemble soprano and alto sections made up of both boys and girls. I strive to have students sing in their most comfortable range. I still spend time expanding and developing their voices in the warm-up process, but they will sing those particular voice parts for the songs. I do stress to them that they aren't altos or sopranos yet. They just happen to be singing these parts for now. By having them sing both parts at the beginning of the year, I've laid the foundation for this idea of not getting locked into a voice part at too young an age.

Grades 7-8 Girls

My 7th and 8th grade girls sing either soprano or alto. I have never had to use a female tenor, and I personally think the practice is unhealthy for two reasons. First, if girls only sing in the tenor range, they will use only the bottom of their range, which can eventually cause some vocal problems. This also prevents them from developing their head voice. The second reason is that it "forces" them to sing with the tone quality of a male. Trying to match the quality of a young man's voice at this age can cause all kinds of stress on a young female voice. I understand why it's done, and I'm not judging anyone who does this. I would just caution you to be very careful with your young, developing voices. Allow them to explore and develop their entire range in a healthy way. Many of my girls do end up singing alto or soprano exclusively for both 7th and 8th grade, but I also have a number of young ladies who will go back and forth from section to section throughout the year.

Since accessing the head voice with consistency is our main goal in 6th grade, we want to develop that head voice in the 7th and 8th grades. We are trying to develop an intense head voice in which they are comfortable singing. Also, the "break" between registers (both lower and upper) can become much more of a problem during these grades. Most girls have a tendency to back off when they are singing in their passaggios. We want them to embrace these areas and not be afraid of what comes out. Another goal for these years is to expand their range. Because most girls at this age are self-conscious (about everything!), we don't always get their "best effort" in their extreme ranges. They don't want to sound "bad" when they sing. (Boys typically don't care about this as much. They know the expectations for them are lower, so they'll sing out no matter how "awful" they think they sound!) It can take years of daily exercises to develop a head voice that is intense and strong, smooth out the passagios, and widen their range.

Boys (in General)

My first recommendation is to read and learn about the male changing voice, especially if you aren't male! I actually don't remember struggling with my own voice change that much. We didn't have much of a choir in middle school, but I did sing. I sang all the way through high school in the concert choir and swing choir (yes, I'm dating myself using the term "swing choir" instead of "show choir"!) I also sang with my dad in our church choir. I'm pretty sure we never warmed-up in our middle school or church choirs. We just got together and rehearsed songs.

I have been singing for as long as I can remember, and it was never a weird activity. I played sports, I sang, and I played drums in a garage band. I was doing what all the other guys my age were doing, and singing wasn't considered uncool. I say all this because I firmly believe that one of the keys to helping men successfully transition through their change is to make singing as normal as possible. If they are trying just as hard at singing as they are at football, basketball, or soccer, they will have an easier time, partly because they won't be afraid to make mistakes or "weird sounds" with their voices. Some of my most successful young male singers are also the school's star athletes. If you can create an atmosphere of trust and respect with a healthy dose of competition, you will be amazed what your men can accomplish. Let's face it—some of the exercises we are going to have them do to help them through their break can be very strange. If they are comfortable in our classroom and feel supported by the class, they'll make some *very* strange sounds...most of them on purpose!

Grade 6 Boys

Our primary goal with 6th grade boys is to get them singing! This singing thing could be new to many of your young men, and they haven't developed the coordination to match pitch very well, much less sing with a beautiful tone. The sooner they find out that singing isn't speaking on pitch, but controlled yelling, the sooner you can start to shape and mold this "sound" into a desirable tone.

One analogy that resonates is that of a pitcher learning to throw a fastball. Let's say the pitcher can throw, with consistent accuracy, a 70-mph fastball. If he tried to throw as hard as he could, his accuracy would suffer, not unlike your young men who sing very loudly! If he only throws 70 mph, he will never develop that 90-mph fastball he'll need at the college level. He has to throw it harder than he can with accuracy to be able to develop the ability to throw it across the plate at a higher velocity. Gradually, by throwing some in the dirt, and even over the backstop, he'll be able to throw harder with more accuracy. Encourage your young men to "throw it in the dirt" as they're learning to control their young voices!

The typical 6th grade boy has an unchanged voice, though I do have exceptions every year. In fact, there seem to be more 6th grade boys every year that are further through their change, but the vast majority are still unchanged. This voice is a beautiful, focused, clear voice with power and a fairly wide range. And, in the right environment, your boys will take more chances than the girls. They'll sing higher, lower, louder, and do all the goofy things we ask them to do to help them become better singers. Our next goal with them, as I mentioned earlier, is to develop their head voice, which becomes the foundation for their changing voice later on. This strong head voice becomes a strong falsetto later on, which will develop into a relaxed head voice even later.

At the beginning of the year, I have all of the boys sing in the same section. They will respond better at this early stage of their singing career if they are with other guys. Plus, they really respond to competition with the girls! (Try to see who can throw a "siren" higher, or crescendo a phrase more, or sing a warm-up faster; whatever it is, your guys will blow the girls away. It might not be the prettiest sound, but the point is to get them taking chances with their voice, and competition is a sneaky way of getting them there.)

I also put the boys together to get them past the awkwardness of singing. They can hear everyone around them struggling with the same issues. Plus, there's power in numbers, and when you get a bunch of boys singing strong together, fasten your seat belts and enjoy the ride! After the first concert, we'll do another voice chart and assign some of them to soprano and the others to alto. Even though many of them are assigned to alto, they are still singing primarily in their head voices because of the literature we use.

So, what about the handful every year who come in with a changing or "changed" voice? I'll get at least one 6th grader each year with an E below the bass clef. Yura was my biggest surprise. He couldn't have been 5 feet tall, but yet could belt out a low E. He didn't have much of a high voice, but wow, what a low voice! For the changing boys who still have what would be considered falsetto at this time, I encourage them to sing in their falsetto. The soprano part is typically easier for these young men because it doesn't lie around the break area, where it can be very difficult to maintain a tone without cracking. If their falsetto doesn't exist (common for a lot of young men whose voices change very rapidly), I will ask them to sing what the rest of their section is singing, but down the octave.

This can be difficult, because most middle school students don't like to be very different from the rest. When you have 80 students singing in their head voices and one singing down the octave, you can hear the poor kid! It takes a lot of encouragement for that young man to be successful. If you're lucky, he'll be the kind of young man who says, "Alright, let's *do* this!" He'll be fine. The opposite of that is the hardest to work with. If you're not careful, and sometimes even if you are, he will start to sing very quietly in monotone, and you could lose him. If you have a few guys who are singing low for whatever reason, put them together and give them the green light to sing low (on pitch) and loudly!

One thing to really listen for is a falsetto voice that tires quickly. I find this with the boys whose voices are changing rapidly, and whose head voices have become falsetto. You can identify this when you hear a "break" in their voice and they sound much breathier in their upper range. They can typically only sing a short time in their falsetto before it tires out. (I always tell these young men that, when going through something for the third or fourth time, they are to audiate instead of sing.) If you're not aware of it, this situation can cause all kinds of tension and vocal issues, so allow them to either rest for a few minutes, or have them drop the octave if they're able. This tiring-out of their falsetto can be a warning sign that your 7th grade boy is getting ready to move from the alto section to the baritone section.

To summarize our discussion of 6th grade boys, the main focus is to get them singing. The secondary focus is to develop a strong, clear head voice. If you've built a foundation of comfortable singing in the upper ranges of your 6th graders, 7th and 8th grade will be easy. Well, relatively!

Grade 7 Boys

In the 7th grade, you will see the widest variety of change in the boys' voices. This is my favorite age to teach for a lot of reasons, but the fact that they are just bizarre every day makes me look forward to coming to school! A 7th grade class is like an amoeba that is constantly changing—it's awesome!

So what do the boys in the 7th grade sound like? Well, they can be sopranos, altos, tenors, *or* basses—and don't forget cambiata, changing 1, changing 2, and changing 3! Some of them will maintain their clear, focused head voices. However, you will notice that many of them are losing their upper range. There is a "husky" or "raspy" quality that starts to creep in that will let you know things are changing. You will start to hear "breaks" from middle C to the F above middle C. This is when the development of the two voices (falsetto and modal/chest voice) begins in most young men. Whether they can maintain a falsetto depends on how quickly their voice changes. You will have young men that totally lose the ability to sing in falsetto. This can last for weeks to over a year. You will also have young men who transition very smoothly through the change, and you'll never hear their voice crack. The typical boy's voice is somewhere in between.

Our main goal with the 7th grade male voice is to establish a foundation of healthy singing that will help make their voice change a natural evolution. Building on the foundation we laid in the 6th grade of developing their head voice is imperative. Still have them sing in their head voice/falsetto daily. But now, in addition, work on a smooth transition between their upper and lower registers. Help them build and strengthen their new "low voice" from the top down. Ultimately, we want grown men with relaxed head voices. (The world doesn't need any more tonsil tenors...please!) This is a very long process for some of our men, taking up to 10 years or longer. Don't expect results tomorrow, or even next year, but continue to work daily in their upper range.

I do three main exercises to help this process. They are found in Section 4 (Exercises 13–15), but they are relevant here while discussing the male changing voice. I do these regularly, but not every day.

 ## Exercise 1:

> This exercise is a siren. Have the boys start low and "throw up" (they love that phrase!) their voice as high and as quickly as they can. Have them come down very slowly, all on an *Ah* vowel. (The vowel you choose is of great debate. I personally can do it easier on *Ah*, and most of my young men are more successful with this as well.)

I will have them throw a frisbee or baseball, or move their hand up and down following their voice to help them "see" it working. I explain that it is the opposite of a roller coaster: you go fast *up* the steep hill, and slowly *down* the less steep hill. I then tell them to focus on three things as they approach the break on the way down:

1. Slow down
2. Open your throat
3. Move more air through

Constant reminders will help them do this exercise without too much cracking.

 ## Exercise 2:

This exercise starts on E above middle C. Have them sing *do-re-mi-fa-so-fa-mi-re-do* on an *Oo* vowel, in falsetto. I start in E major because, of the boys who have falsetto, most of them will be able to sing in this key as opposed to a lower key. Ascend to around C major, dropping the baritones out around A major, and drop the alto boys out around C major.

 ## Exercise 3:

This exercise is the toughest. It is a descending major scale, on the vowel *Ah*, starting around B above middle C. They will start in their falsetto (if they have one) and on the way down will "let" their voice change when it tells them to. Many of them will drop an octave as their voice breaks. That's ok, because that tells us they aren't "muscling" the notes to make them come out. With a lot of work, that transition will become smooth, and then they will be able to develop that easy head voice that we so desire from them.

These exercises aren't exclusive to 7th graders, but this is the grade in which I use them the most. I do them regularly with my 8th graders, and I have done them with my high school students too. Have the girls sing along with the boys, because these are great exercises for them as well.

Where you place your 7th grade boys will depend on whether you are directing an all-male ensemble or a mixed group. Books on the adolescent male voice expound upon the various classifications of the changing voice. Some list up to six states of change. Many suggest that you should move the boys into sections based on the stage they are in. This is where all of the reading we do on the male changing voice can cause confusion when applying it to practical situations. This research was done so that we, as choir directors, may be more successful when working with these young men. Thankfully, the days of having boys stop singing when their voices "break" are over! But from a realistic viewpoint, the chances that you will be splitting your 7th grade choir into six parts to accommodate each category of the changing male voice are slim at best. Plus, there isn't much music written in six parts for 7th grade students. Practically, then, what can we do with all of these different voices?

If this is an **all-male** choir, and it is all 7th grade boys, your choices are fairly easy. Most music written for this age is tenor/bass, tenor/tenor/bass or tenor/baritone/bass. However, it's important to understand that these young men aren't actually "tenors" or "basses." As stated earlier, some are soprano and alto, some are cambiata, and some really do have "bass" notes. Since most of the publishers are putting out TB, TTB, and TBB music, our job is to find the most comfortable section for each boy. The good news is that much of the music being arranged today has these young men in mind. The ranges tend to be more moderate, allowing the young men to sing in their comfortable range. The tenor part tends to lie higher than would be comfortable for a mature tenor, and the bass part doesn't lie too low or have too low of a tessitura.

A fairly large number of your 7th grade boys will sound unchanged, and will still have a clear tone quality while ascending into the meat of the treble clef and higher. You won't notice any break as they ascend or descend. Their most comfortable range in which to sing is around middle C up to the G or A above middle C. These young men will be most successful singing in the tenor section. Most will have a lowest note right at 4th-line F in the bass clef. Their part is written in the treble clef, to be sung an octave lower than written.

You will also have a number of young men whose voices are starting to get "husky," and you might start hearing a slight break around middle C. The higher notes are becoming more difficult for them, and their high voice is starting to resemble a falsetto. Many of them will still only have 4th-line F in the bass clef as their lowest note, but some may be able to sing to the D below that. The middle part would be the best fit for these boys, whether it's labeled tenor or baritone. The range doesn't sit too high or too low. If they sing too high for long periods of time, they will tire very easily. Trying to sing too low will cause them vocal tension, and could be potentially harmful.

There is also a group of young men who sound mostly changed. Many of them will have 1st-line G in the bass clef or lower. Some will only be able to sing as low as 2nd-line B in the bass clef. Most will have the ability to sing up to middle C, but not all of them. You will now hear a very distinct break in most of their voices around middle C. Some will have no voice at all above that. Those who do have a falsetto will sound fairly breathy and again will tire very quickly singing in that register. The bass part will fit most of these young men very well.

On the other hand, if your ensemble happens to be **mixed**, you will have fewer choices of where to place your 7th grade boys. One big problem with boys in choir tends to be numbers. There just don't seem to be enough of them! To get the most out of the boys you have, consider using 3-part mixed music, which is written for soprano, alto, and baritone. This "baritone" part has the range of about a 6th, usually from 4th-line F in the bass clef up to D above middle C. For about half of your young men, this is a very comfortable range in which to sing on a daily basis.

Most of the rest of your boys (the more unchanged voices) will be more comfortable singing higher. What makes the most sense for these boys, based on the earlier description (a comfortable range from middle C to G or A above that), is to have them sing alto. This means that your girls will be divided approximately 60% soprano and 40% alto, depending on the number of boys you have singing alto. You will likely have a few of your boys who could sing soprano (and probably stronger and clearer than most of your girls!), but there is power in numbers. In a mixed choir, your boys will still want to be together as much as possible, no matter how supportive an atmosphere you have created. Consider sitting your baritones next to the alto section so the alto men can be right next to the other men.

Not every 7th grade male voice will fit nicely into these sections, and you may still need to help these few boys with octave displacement here and there. This is where voice charting really helps. For example, your young men can look at their lowest note on their voice chart and the lowest note in the score and see if they will have issues. You can help them by marking alternative notes in their scores (and yours) that they will sing instead of the written notes. This simple task will help keep them more engaged, as we know what happens when our 7th grade boys are not engaged in a lesson!

Grade 8 Boys

In the 8th grade, you will again have young men who sing soprano, alto, tenor, and bass, though there will be fewer who can sing soprano or alto. On the surface, many of your 8th graders will sound like high school men. This is deceiving, and you will need to be careful selecting literature so as not to push them beyond what they are capable. Their basic ranges and sound are not unlike the 7th graders; they just have more body to their voices. You will also notice more young men with bigger trouble spots. You'll hear bigger breaks, less falsetto, more who sing way too low in a monotone voice, and more who generally have difficulty matching pitch. The obvious root to all of these "problems," of course, is that their bodies are changing so much and so quickly. Even athletically, they can be less coordinated, so it's no wonder they are having trouble coordinating all of the intricate muscles it takes to sing on pitch! I've found that those who still have a falsetto (and that's most of them) can still sing very accurately in that voice, even if they aren't as accurate in their low voice. However, they will tire quickly up there.

In an **all-male** ensemble, the placement would be the same as for your 7th grade men's choir. You will end up with fewer tenors and more basses, but the majority will be singing baritone or tenor 2. There will be more literature from which to choose because your basses will have a lower comfortable range than your 7th graders, and the tenors (most still altos or cambiata) will mostly have retained their easy high range.

If your 8th grade ensemble is **mixed**, I recommend that you place your men in either the tenor section or bass section. Appropriate SATB literature for these voices is very easy to find. There is increasingly more 3-part mixed with optional baritone music available as well. You will find that the bass part lies in a comfortable range for most of the young basses, and the tenor part still doesn't go too far below the 4th-line F of the bass clef. Not to belabor a point, but I can't emphasize it enough: your men will be more successful, and will want to participate fully, if they are given music in which they can sing most, if not all, of the pitches. This is where SAB music becomes problematic. The baritone part is typically too low for the young tenors, and too high for the young basses. Re-writing is then a must. The better option is finding that appropriate SATB literature for young voices. Even if your young men are grossly outnumbered by the ladies, they will be able to balance more successfully if the music "fits" their voices. If your men can't sing a part because it is out of their range, they will get bored or frustrated. Either one is a recipe for disaster in the middle school classroom!

I have two goals for my young men in 8th grade. The first is to continue developing their head voices and to smooth out their break area. The other is to start developing a relaxed lower range. The big mistake boys make when first learning to sing low is using too much "muscle." When I hear them trying to push the notes from their throat, I talk about how the opposite of "muscle" in the sound is "air." I'm not after a breathy tone, but rather an open throat. If we can develop a lower range with "air" as the foundation, they will be able to add more strength without tension as they mature into their adult voice—a much healthier approach.

There are many exercises that can develop and promote this technique. Here are two with which I have found much success. They are Exercises 5 and 3 in Section 4, but I have included them here for a more thorough description.

 # Exercise 1:

This exercise will help boys maintain a forward focus (in the mask) as they descend.

Then have them try to maintain that feel as they open to the *Ah* and sing the rest of the exercise. I would start this in the middle range, around F major, and descend to around G major or lower, depending on how low my basses can sing. Everyone starts the exercise, and I will have the sopranos, altos, and tenors drop out at various times.

 # Exercise 2:

Another good exercise for developing a relaxed lower range is the lip trill.

The lip trill does two important things. First, it makes singers focus their energy to the lips and the abdominal area, hopefully keeping the rest of their vocal mechanism relaxed. Second, to maintain the lip trill, you have to maintain steady air pressure from the abs. If you have too much or too little pressure, you will lose the trill. After they are comfortable with the lip trill and can maintain a consistent tone, have them open to an *Ee* or *Ah* on the third note of the exercise. Singers should maintain the steady pressure and forward focus. Over time this will help your young men develop a relaxed sound in their lower range.

Section 2
Basic Warm-Up Outline

There are as many approaches to the beginning of choir rehearsal as there are directors. There are quite a few classifications of warm-ups also. For the purpose of this book, the following classification will be used:

    I.   Physical Movement/Stretching

    II.   Breathing

    III.   Warming Down

    IV.   Warming Up

    V.   Specialized

This daily warm-up outline covers the important bases for vocal development and rehearsal preparation. While it is a brief explanation, it gives you an idea of my approach.

I. Physical Movement/Stretching

As previously mentioned, I approach singing as an athletic activity in which the entire body is involved. We all have our "favorite" stretching activities. Some directors like to put music on while the students stretch, some lead the stretching, some have students lead, and others let the students do what works for them. I don't claim that the stretching exercises my choirs do are perfect, but there are a few very important characteristics of which you should be aware.

A stretching warm-up should work the entire body. Try not to spend too much time on one part of the body or ignore something else. The following is what I use in my classroom every day as our stretching routine.

1.   Raise your hands above your head, palms facing up with interlocked fingers. Pull from side to side, stretching the sides of the body. Do this 4–6 times, unlock your fingers, raise up on your toes, and "push

the ceiling up" with your hands. Slowly relax, feeling all of the tension release from your body.

2. Twist your torso from side to side with your arms bent at the elbows. It's important to keep your head forward and not twist too far, so as not to put any undue stress on your knees.

3. Roll your shoulders, making big circles from the front to the back. After finishing the last one, you should be standing tall with a raised rib cage. (To add some fun, have your students try squares, triangles on their points, and triangles on their bases. Then start naming random shapes to see how they do. Octagons are a favorite with my students!)

4. Roll your head, being careful not to roll all the way around. (Rolling one's head all the way around places unnecessary stress on the neck and spine, doing potential harm.) Drop your chin to your chest, roll to one side and stop. Repeat, rolling to the other side and stopping. Do this 3–5 times.

5. Depending on the age and maturity level of the choir, we rub shoulders and the back of the neck. My 6th and 7th graders rub their own shoulders and neck. Our 8th graders turn from side to side and rub their neighbor's neck and shoulders. Of course, I am careful to explain the do's and don'ts of this activity. After a few days of awkwardness, they start to understand the importance of it.

During the entire stretching process, you need to ensure that *all* of your students are participating fully and correctly. Every student needs to try their hardest and do their best. This lays the foundation for your expectations, not only for the rest of the warm-up, but for the rest of the rehearsal. I would also recommend stretching in silence. Try it and see how their focus changes!

II. Breathing

This is an opportunity to focus on the breathing process without any phonation. Allow me to briefly explain breathing for singing as I present it to my middle schoolers. (This is at least a chapter's worth of information that I'm putting into a few sentences. If this is new, or if you need more specific explanation, consider taking a vocal pedagogy class or private voice lessons.)

When the body needs oxygen, the diaphragm drops and the lungs expand. When the diaphragm drops, it displaces all of the organs below it, including the stomach, intestines, gall bladder, etc. Since these internal organs can't go down too far, they go down and out, and the abdomen area expands. I have my students think of their rib cage as the walls of a building, and their diaphragm as the floor. The strength and foundation of a building is in the walls, not the floor. A building can stand without a floor, but not without walls. Students start with an expanded (raised) rib cage and maintain it as they inhale and exhale. I have them place one hand on their sternum and the other hand just below the belly button. Then, as they breathe, the hand on their rib cage should remain still, while the lower hand moves out on inhalation and in on exhalation.

I also use a weight-lifting analogy. A weight-lifter works with weights against the natural relaxation tendencies of the muscles (they flex, then relax), similar to a diaphragm dropping (flexing) and rising with resistance (relaxing). The flexing of the abdominal muscles during this exhalation (or phonation) part of the process simulates the use of weights. We know that we have very little (if any) control over our diaphragm, but students will feel more support if they think of working against the natural relaxation of the diaphragm.

Here is an exercise to try with your students to help them feel the correct breathing process. Have them lie with their backs on the floor. Place a stack of books (e.g. 3–4 textbooks) on their belly, below their belly button. Their goal is to make the books move (rise) when they inhale. Demonstrate in class by having one of your students lie on a piano bench. They love to volunteer, especially in hopes of being the star that "raised the books!"

Additional exercises with a focus on breathing can be found in Section 4.

III. Warming Down

Not to be confused with what an athlete does at the end of a workout, "warming down" describes the direction of your first exercises of the rehearsal. After the breathing mechanism has been engaged through breathing exercises, these warm-down exercises encourage the students to sing with a more relaxed sound. The focus of these exercises should be an easy, but well-supported sound.

There are many basic, descending exercises that work well as a first vocal exercise of the day. One of my favorites is having students start in their middle range and sing a 5-note descending pattern on a lip trill, or *Oo* vowel shape. (The middle of their range is different for all grade levels, and I will be addressing this later in the book.) As they are descending, be mindful of where you are pitch-wise, and be ready to drop out certain voice parts. Depending on the length of the rehearsal, and what time of year it is, I may do 1–3 descending exercises.

IV. Warming Up

This is exactly what it says: warming up the upper range. There are countless exercises for this purpose. Make sure you find one that has range expansion as its main function. Don't pick one that has too many other purposes built-in, such as placement, bounce, or vowel shape. Remember, you are dealing with young voices that have limited focus. If you give them only one or two things to think about and work on at a time, they will be more successful. Again, depending on the time of year and the length of rehearsal, I might pick one or two different warming-up exercises.

V. Specialized

These are the exercises to build and develop the vocal/choral instrument. This would include exercises that focus on:

    a) Bounce/Support

    b) Diction/Articulation

    c) Choral/Intonation

    d) Resonance/Placement

    e) Tone Quality

    f) Flexibility/Dynamics

    g) Register Transitions/Passaggios

When I try to categorize vocal exercises, they all seem to fall into these basic categories. There are other methods for categorization, but for the sake of this book, we'll stick with these seven. The number I use depends on what music we're working on at the time, or what area of the voice/choir we're trying to develop.

So, we have discussed why we should vocalize our students, and we have a basic outline of what the warm-up time might look like. What next? Well, sometimes it's important to find out what *not* to do before we get started on what to do.

Section 3
Common Mistakes

The biggest mistake we can make as directors is to not be fully aware of *all* of the students. This isn't just for warm-ups, but for the entire rehearsal. To boil it all down, a choir director is responsible for four main things:

1. **Watch** students for correct posture, vowel formation, tension, behavior, level of engagement, etc.

2. **Remind** students to use correct posture, to breathe low, etc.

3. **Adjust** students if they don't correct themselves after being reminded.

4. **Push** students to do their best.

If you pay attention to each of these areas in each rehearsal, it's a **WRAP**! (Hopefully the acronym will help remind you of the steps.) We are trying to develop self-motivated young learners. Nurturing a self-motivated student is one of our goals in teaching. This is a 13-year process that starts in Kindergarten. When we get them in middle school, they are at one of the most crucial ages, as well as one of the most difficult. My 7th and 8th graders need as many (or more) reminders as my 6th graders, but for different reasons. The 6th graders still want to please. The 8th graders may finally be able to see the good that we're doing for them individually.

This concept of watching, reminding, adjusting, and pushing them applies to everything we do with middle school students. Do you want them to be good citizens? Watch them, remind them, adjust them, and push them, and you will see results. Above all, be patient with them. It takes time to develop all of the skills we're talking about, so you can't expect great changes overnight!

The following common mistakes deal with the warm-up process and are more general concerns. We will deal with specific issues involving each warm-up in Section 4.

Physical Movement/Stretching

1. Not stretching at all would be a big mistake. The students need this time to get focused individually and collectively. They also need to get their bodies physically ready for this full-body, athletic activity we call singing.

2. Letting the students do their own stretching can also be a mistake if they don't know what they're doing. Some stretching can actually do more harm than good, or cause tension where we don't want it. This includes rolling your head all the way around in the back, or not keeping your head forward as you twist your torso.

Breathing

1. Not requiring the students to have their hands on their sternum and abdomen will make it more difficult for them to check if they are breathing properly.

2. When the students look around the room, they have a tendency to move as they hiss/sing. Not keeping a focus point can create inconsistent breath support, and in turn, an inconsistent tone.

Warm-Ups

1. The first and biggest warming-up mistake that I've witnessed is **starting in the wrong key**. For example, don't make C major your "default" key. I've met very few new baritones who can sing comfortably in C major! The starting key for a warm-up changes with each grade level, gender, and warm-up.

2. Another common mistake is **keeping everyone singing through the entire exercise**. Have students drop out and re-enter as their voice tells them. This is one of the reasons why we chart our students' voices 3–4 times each year. They have a voice chart that shows them their highest and lowest notes on the staff and on the keyboard, so they will know when they should stop singing. Voice charting also helps *you* get to know their voices so you can do the same thing for them.

   As your choir is singing a descending exercise, for example, it will be important for you to know when to have just your new 7th grade baritones drop out while everyone else continues singing. You will bring these baritones back in with the rest of the choir, but in their upper range, later in the exercise. This technique allows all students the opportunity to increase their range. This also keeps these young baritones on their toes, knowing that they will be joining the rest of the group soon, and will be expected to pick it up again where they left off.

3. **Using exercises with a range of an octave or more** can also be troublesome for developing voices. Most of us sang warm-ups with our college voice teacher, or in our college choir, that had a range of more than one octave. This type of exercise won't prove too difficult for a 6th grade class that is made up of girls and primarily unchanged boys voices, but students may have a difficult time maneuvering through the different registers and over their breaks. However, wide-ranged exercises will prove more troublesome for the 7th–8th grade young men who are in various stages of change, some with no notes lower than F below middle C, and others with nothing above middle C!

   As an example, let's take a typical 7th grade choir. Most of your young men can sing the F below middle C, and that's their lowest note. This means that the top note of the exercise will be the F above that. Now picture most of your 7th grade girls with their relatively breathy voices singing their high F! This one octave is difficult enough; start moving it up or down and you'll lose singers. This isn't to say that you can't do any exercises that have the range of an octave. A favorite of my students is Exercise 23 in Section 4:

   > *do*
   >
   > *do–re–do*
   >
   > *do–re–mi–re–do*
   >
   > *do–re–mi–fa–mi–re–do*
   >
   > Etc.

   This is a great exercise in the right key. Plus, you don't move it up or down.

4. Remember that "**one size does not fit all**." What works perfectly for your 6th graders may not work at all for your 7th graders, and vice versa. Don't be afraid to modify an exercise that isn't working like you think it should.

5. **Going the wrong direction** with an exercise can be detrimental. Most exercises have a direction (ascending or descending) that makes sense, especially with younger voices. Exercise 3 in Section 4, for example, should be used as a descending exercise. Trying to start that exercise too high on the *Ng* could cause tension in a young developing voice. An advanced high school student or college vocalist should be able to sing this exercise in their upper range without a problem, but a young singer

who is still developing good breathing and support habits would have problems singing this without tension in their upper range.

6. Finally, **combining too many purposes** into one exercise can be very confusing for your students. Try to remember the many layers of activities that we want them to do every time they open their mouths to sing. We could say posture is one layer, but for them it's many layers! Are their feet shoulder-width apart? Are their knees slightly bent? Are their arms at their sides? Is their rib cage expanded? Are their shoulders back and relaxed? Is their head level? (By the way, I call these the Six Steps of Good Posture for Singing, and my students are tested on them.) Then add correct breathing, which most of your 6th graders probably just learned how to do. How about mouth position? You get the point.

Let's make their job easier and give them exercises with few purposes. Or, only focus on one of the many functions of an exercise. After a week or so, you can add that next purpose. The more elements students have to think about, the less we tend to get from them. It's overwhelming! The less students have to focus on, the quicker they can "perfect" a concept, and the sooner we can add another layer.

We want our students to be successful. Study every exercise you use. Spend time figuring out the purpose and function of every exercise you do. Sing each exercise yourself to see how, or if, it fits and works. If you can't find a purpose, don't use it. Remember, we are building beautiful, healthy voices. There are many, many books out there full of vocal exercises for your choir and for your voice students. Many of them even tell you the purpose of each exercise. (I have provided a list of resources I have found valuable at the back of this book.)

Figuring out what these common mistakes were involved a lot of trial and error...LOTS of error! Look for signs such as body tension, confusion, or a lack of engagement. Listen for signs like vocal tension, dropping the octave, or dropping out altogether. Use your instincts, and you can avoid many of these mistakes up front.

Section 4
Warm-Ups

I am going to walk you through the warm-up process, including why I select and how I modify a warm-up for each grade level. When I present at conferences, I often ask for favorite warm-ups from the attendees and then demonstrate what I would do with them. For purposes of this book, I'll take you through some of *my* favorite warm-ups, grade-by-grade, and hopefully you can see the method behind my madness. It may seem difficult to keep track of at first, but by using these exercises and being aware of where you are pitch-wise, the process will get easier and make more sense. Then you will be able to apply these principles to your own favorites.

The secrets to successfully warming-up your middle school choir involve *key, range,* and *direction.* (I touched on each of these in Section 3.) The key in which you start an exercise is paramount to success. All of your students need to be able to sing the pitches, at least initially. As you progress through an exercise, it will get too high or too low for some of your singers. This is when you need to know and understand their ranges, so you can drop them out and bring them back in at the correct pitch level. Finally, know your warm-ups, and know which direction each one should go. If you take a descending exercise and ascend with it, you are setting your students up for failure and potential vocal problems.

I tried to help you avoid common mistakes by listing some "Tips for Success" at the end of each exercise. These should help you anticipate any issues before they arise.

The warm-ups are not in sequential order, so don't start with Exercise 1 and work your way through to the last one. They have been designed so that you can open the book, select what you need, and follow the directions as you warm-up your choir. Please practice playing and singing them before you introduce them to your choir. Think about how you study choral literature before selecting it and introducing it to your choir. Similarly, you have to really know an exercise inside and out before your choir can be successful with it.

Enjoy!

Exercise 1

Purpose: breathing; breath control

This basic breathing exercise focuses on the process of correct breathing and the development of breath control. Have students place one hand on their sternum (this hand doesn't move) and the other hand on their abdomen, just below their belly button (this hand moves). Then have them do this 5-step process:

1. Find a focal point with their eyes. (This can be a poster on the wall, or something on the board at which they will stare the entire time. Ideally, you want them to feel like they are drilling a hole into the item of focus.)

2. Raise their rib cage. (Have them keep it raised for the duration of the exercise. The hand is there to make sure it doesn't move.)

3. Exhale. (The rib cage should not have moved, but the lower hand should have moved in.)

4. Inhale. (Again, the rib cage should not move, but the lower hand should move out quite a bit, and down slightly.)

5. Hiss/Lip trill/Phonate. (They should feel a "tightening" with the lower hand, and then it will start to move in slowly as they hiss, but the rib cage should not drop.)

Using these five steps, work them through this chart of inhalation and hissing/phonating. The pulse should be somewhere around 70 beats per minute.

	Inhale	Hiss/Lip trill/Phonate (any vowel)
Counts:	4	12
	4	16
	4	20
	4	24
	2	12
	2	16
	2	20
	2	24
	2	28
	1	12
	1	16
	1	etc.

Do no more than three rows of the chart a day, since controlled breathing exercises can lead to light-headed students! Beginning the year with 4 beats of inhaling and 8 beats of hissing is a good starting point, even for your 7th and 8th grade choirs. Gradually work through this chart, with some skipping around as needed. Have the students keep track of when they run out of air, so they can see their progress. Of course, students love competitions, so occasionally have them sit when they run out of air to see who's the last one standing. (Please make sure they are standing in front of a chair!)

6th Grade:

- Perform the pitched exercises on F or G above middle C. It's important that students are in their head voices.
- Allow them more time between exercises at the start of the year.

7th Grade:

- Perform the pitched exercises on G or A with the sopranos and altos singing in the same octave (above middle C), and the young baritones singing an octave lower.

8th Grade:

- Perform the pitched exercises on F or G with the sopranos and altos singing in the same octave (above middle C), and the tenors and basses in unison an octave lower.

Tips for Success:

- Watch students' upper hands (placed on their sternum) for movement, and remind them to keep them still.
- If you have students who find the lip trill difficult, you can have them roll their R's instead. If they can't do that either, have them put one index finger on the middle of each cheek and push slightly forward, toward their lips. This will relax their lips, helping them to make the lip trill happen.

 ## Exercise 2

Purpose: breath control and support

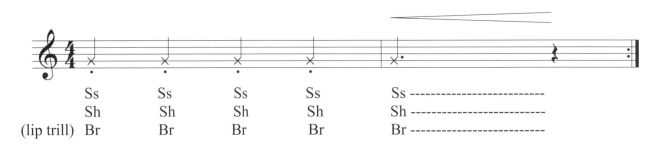

This is a great breath support/control exercise. It will help students learn how to engage their abdominal muscles in the singing process.

They will inhale, pulse the first four beats with their abs ($\quarternote = 70$), and then "push" the rest of their air out over the next three beats. They have one beat in which to inhale before they repeat. Repeat three times, for a total of four times, trying to crescendo more each time.

All Grades:

- Perform the exercise on one breath.
- Only do 3–4 at a time.

Tips for Success:

- Watch for correct breathing technique throughout the exercise.

- Don't do more than 3–4 repetitions at a time during one warm-up session. Students may become light-headed.

- If you have students who find the lip trill difficult, you can have them roll their R's instead. If they can't do that either, have them put one index finger on the middle of each cheek and push slightly forward, toward their lips. This will relax their lips, helping them to make the lip trill happen.

 *Exercise 3*

Purpose: warm-down; beginning phonation; support; tone quality

Oo _____
Brr _____
Brr _____   Ee/Ah _____

This excellent "warm-down" exercise is also a great exercise for the first month of the school year. Have your students sing on *Oo* for a few weeks to help develop a uniform vowel shape. This can also help them develop a "heady" tone, as opposed to the "chesty" sound that many of them are accustomed to using.

Later, after they are comfortable with the *Oo*, introduce the lip trill. (This will be sooner for the 7th and 8th grades than for the 6th grade.) The lip trill does two important things. First, it makes students focus their energy away from the vocal mechanism to the lips and abdominal area, while keeping the rest of their vocal mechanism relaxed. Second, to maintain the lip trill, you have to maintain steady air pressure from the abs. If there is too much or too little pressure, you will lose the trill. This helps students develop a very consistent energized tone when singing. When working with the older students, consider alternating back and forth between the *Oo* and the lip trill on different days.

6th Grade:

- Start in the key of F Major (above middle C), making sure students are in their head voices.
- Boys and girls sing in the same octave.
- Descend by ½ steps.
- Stop around C or B♭ Major.

7th Grade:

- Start in the key of G Major.
- Sopranos and altos sing in unison (above middle C); baritones sing an octave lower.
- Descend by ½ steps.
- Baritones stop singing around F (below middle C).
- Sopranos and altos continue descending by ½ steps.
- Baritones join again (in unison with the sopranos and altos) around B♭ Major.
- Continue descending by ½ steps.
- Ladies stop singing around A♭ Major.
- Men continue descending until F Major.

8th Grade:

- Start in the key of G Major.
- Sopranos and altos sing in unison (above middle C); tenors and basses sing in unison an octave lower.
- Descend by ½ steps.
- Tenors stop singing around E Major (below middle C).
- Sopranos, altos, and basses continue descending by ½ steps.
- Tenors join again (in unison with the sopranos and altos) around B♭ Major.
- All continue descending until around G Major.

Tips for Success:

- Make sure the ladies and unchanged boys start in their head voices.
- This is a descending exercise. Avoid ascending by ½ steps.
- Start the exercise high enough for your young tenors and baritones to be able to sing the initial lower notes.
- Perform at a slow tempo ($\quarternote$ = 44–50).

Exercise 4

Purpose: warm-down; beginning phonation; placement

Ng ————————

This exercise helps your singers develop a relaxed lower range. It is also a great exercise to help them get their tone focused into the mask. (The "mask" is the area on the face—including the cheek bones, bridge of the nose, and the forehead right above the eyes—where we feel the tone sit. Think of the Lone Ranger's mask!)

The *Ng* is the same sound as the end of the word "sung." Have them say "sung" and hold the last sound *Nnnnng* to get used to the feel. For the first few weeks of doing this exercise, have the students put their index fingers on the bridge of their nose to feel the resonance. This will help them develop the feeling of singing into the mask.

6th Grade:

- Start in the key of G Major.
- Boys and girls sing in unison (above middle C).
- Descend by ½ steps.
- Stop around C Major.

7th Grade:

- Start in the key of G Major.
- Sopranos and altos sing in unison (above middle C); baritones sing an octave lower.
- Descend by ½ steps.
- Baritones stop singing around E Major (below middle C).
- Sopranos and altos continue descending by ½ steps.
- Baritones join again (in unison with the sopranos and altos) around B♭ Major.
- Continue descending by ½ steps.
- Ladies stop singing around A♭ Major.
- Men continue descending until F Major.

8th Grade:

- Start in the key of G Major.
- Sopranos and altos sing in unison, and tenors and basses sing in unison an octave lower.
- Descend by ½ steps.
- Tenors stop singing around E Major (below middle C).
- Sopranos, altos, and basses continue descending by ½ steps.
- Tenors join again (in unison with the sopranos and altos) around B♭ Major.
- Continue descending until A♭ or G Major.

Tips for Success:

- Make sure the ladies and unchanged boys start in their head voices.
- This is a descending exercise. Avoid ascending by ½ steps.
- Since the *Ng* is rather closed, starting too high can cause tension in young voices.
- Perform at a relaxed tempo ($\quarternote$ = 60–70).

Exercise 5

Purpose: warm-down; placement

This warm-down exercise is an extension of Exercise 4. As discussed earlier, it works very well to help your singers develop a relaxed lower range. It is also a great exercise to help them get their tone focused into the mask. The *Ng* is the same sound as the end of the word "sung." Have them say "sung" and hold the last sound *Nnnnng* to get used to the feel.

Since this exercise is a little more advanced than Exercise 4, try having them put their index fingers on the bridge of their nose and their thumbs on their cheekbones to feel the resonance. This will help them develop the feeling of singing into the "mask." The challenge is to feel the buzz on the bridge of their nose and their cheekbones when they sing the *Ng*. With much work, the students may be able to maintain the buzz on the *Ah*. This is a fairly advanced technique, so don't let them get frustrated!

6th Grade:

- Start in the key of G Major.
- Boys and girls sing in unison (above middle C).
- Descend by ½ steps.
- Stop around C Major.

7th Grade:

- Start in the key of G Major.
- Sopranos and altos sing in unison (above middle C); baritones sing an octave lower.
- Descend by ½ steps.
- Baritones stop singing around E Major (below middle C).
- Sopranos and altos continue descending by ½ steps.
- Baritones join again (in unison with the sopranos and altos) around B♭ Major.
- Continue descending by ½ steps.
- Ladies stop singing around A♭ Major.
- Men continue descending until F Major.

8th Grade:

- Start in the key of G Major.
- Sopranos and altos sing in unison, and tenors and basses sing in unison an octave lower.
- Descend by ½ steps.
- Tenors stop singing around E Major (below middle C).
- Sopranos, altos and basses continue descending by ½ steps.
- Tenors join again (in unison with the sopranos and altos) around B♭ Major.
- Continue descending until A♭ or G Major.

Tips for Success:

- Make sure the ladies and unchanged boys start in their head voices.
- This is a descending exercise. Avoid ascending by ½ steps.
- Since the *Ng* is rather closed, starting too high can cause tension in young voices.
- Perform at a relaxed tempo (♩ = 60–70).

 *Exercise 6*

Purpose: warm-down; tone quality

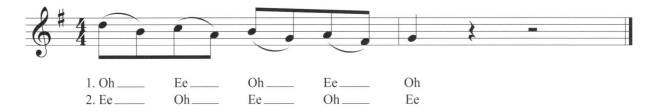

1. Oh____	Ee____	Oh____	Ee____	Oh
2. Ee____	Oh____	Ee____	Oh____	Ee

This is another descending exercise that works well as a warm-down. Since the difficulty level is greater than the previous warm-down exercises, you will want to start this a few weeks into the school year with your beginners, and sometime during week 2 with the other grades. It's a great exercise to develop round, consistent vowels. Most of the focus should be spent matching vowel shapes.

To manually create the correct vowel, have students put one index finger on each corner of their mouth, hold them about 2 inches apart, and push forward slightly to achieve rounded lips. Their job is to use their tongue to change the vowels while maintaining rounded, narrow lips. The tip of the tongue should touch the back of the bottom front teeth, and the rest of the tongue moves up (Ee) and down (Oh) to produce the correct vowel sound. The jaw should remain still, not moving up and down with the tongue.

6th Grade:

- Start in the key of G Major.
- Boys and girls sing in unison (above middle C).
- Descend by ½ steps.
- Stop around C Major.

7th Grade:

- Start in the key of G Major.
- Sopranos and altos sing in unison (above middle C); baritones sing an octave lower.
- Descend by ½ steps.
- Baritones stop singing around E Major (below middle C).
- Sopranos and altos continue descending by ½ steps.
- Baritones join again (in unison with the sopranos and altos) around B♭ Major.
- Continue descending by ½ steps.
- Ladies stop singing around A♭ Major.
- Men continue descending until F Major.

8th Grade:

- Start in the key of G Major.
- Sopranos and altos sing in unison, and tenors and basses sing in unison (an octave lower).
- Descend by ½ steps.
- Tenors stop singing around E Major (below middle C).
- Sopranos, altos, and basses continue descending by ½ steps.
- Tenors join again (in unison with the sopranos and altos) around B♭ Major.
- Continue descending until A or A♭ Major.

Tips for Success:

- This is a descending exercise. Avoid ascending by ½ steps.
- To start on a round *Oh*, have the choir inhale with an *Oh*-shaped mouth.
- Focus on round, consistent vowel shapes.
- Watch their jaws for movement, and correct if necessary.
- Once students are successful with their fingers on the corners of their mouths, have them perform it without their fingers.

Exercise 7

Purpose: warm-up; placement; diction; tone quality

Mee	oh	mee	oh	mee	oh	mee	oh	mee	oh	mee	oh	mee
Zee	oh	zee	oh	zee	oh	zee	oh	zee	oh	zee	oh	zee
Vee	oh	vee	oh	vee	oh	vee	oh	vee	oh	vee	oh	vee
Thee	oh	thee	oh	thee	oh	thee	oh	thee	oh	thee	oh	thee

This exercise utilizes different voiced consonants and only two different vowels. It's similar to Exercise 6, but more involved. The vowels change every eighth note instead of every beat. Also, the addition of the consonants makes it difficult to maintain the basic *Oh* shape of Exercise 6. 6th graders should not attempt this exercise until they have a good grasp on Exercise 6.

I would introduce this exercise without the consonants. Have the students sing it slowly at first to ensure that they are singing the vowels correctly. Then add one consonant (Mm), and have them speak it in rhythm. After this, they can slowly begin singing, making sure they are maintaining round, narrow vowel shapes. This is not a range expansion exercise, so it should be done in the middle of their range, changing consonants every 4th or 5th repetition.

6th Grade:

- Start in the key of G Major.
- Boys and girls sing in unison (above middle C).
- Descend by ½ steps to around E♭ Major.
- Ascend by ½ steps to around G Major.
- Descend and ascend again as needed to work your way through the various consonants (4–5 times for each consonant).

7th Grade:

- Start in the key of G Major.
- Sopranos and altos sing in unison (above middle C); baritones sing an octave lower.
- Descend by ½ steps to around E Major.
- Ascend by ½ steps to around A♭ Major.
- Descend and ascend again as needed to work your way through the various consonants (4–5 times for each consonant).

8th Grade:

- Start in the key of G Major.
- Sopranos and altos in unison, and tenors and basses in unison (an octave lower).
- Descend by ½ steps to around E♭ Major.
- Ascend by ½ steps to around A Major.
- Descend and ascend again as needed to work your way through the various consonants (4–5 times for each consonant).

Tips for Success:

- Start in a comfortable key that's not too high.
- Stay within a moderate range. This is not a range expansion exercise.
- Focus on the placement of their tone and their vowel shapes.
- Don't use too many different voiced consonants (they don't all work well, such as *L*).
- Watch for excessive jaw movement. A little movement is fine, but don't let it get in the way of excellent vowel shapes.

 *Exercise 8*

Purpose: warm-up; vowel uniformity; tone quality

Oh ____   Ee ____   Oh ____   Ee ____   Oh

This exercise is similar to Exercise 6 in that it uses the same vowel combination and the same intervals. As with that exercise, make sure that students have uniform, rounded vowel shapes.

Another technique to help develop rounded vowel shapes, other than placing the fingers on the corners of the mouth, is to have students put the heel of their hand on their chin, hold the chin in place (being careful not to press down on the jaw), place the thumb and index finger on the corners of the mouth, and push forward slightly to round the lips. This will help them feel any movement in the lips or jaw, and allow them to focus on only tongue movement. After your students have created a certain amount of muscle memory with this, they can drop the hand.

This is an ascending warm-up exercise, but be careful to not go too high early in the year. Sense how your choir is handling the higher notes of the exercise, and gradually increase the range as the year goes on. Young treble voices can easily sing G above the treble clef by middle/late in the year with a good amount of freedom in their tone.

6th Grade:

- Start in the key of E♭ Major.
- Boys and girls sing in unison (above middle C).
- Ascend by ½ steps.
- Continue until B♭ –C Major.

7th Grade:

- Start in the key of E Major.
- Sopranos and altos sing in unison (above middle C); baritones sing an octave lower.
- Ascend by ½ steps.
- Drop out the male altos around A Major (or have them drop the octave).
- Encourage the young baritones to sing lightly as they ascend into their head voices.
- Continue until C–D Major.

8th Grade:

- Start in the key of D Major (the tenors may need to wait for a couple of reps before joining).
- Sopranos and altos sing in unison, and the tenors and basses sing in unison (an octave lower).
- Ascend by ½ steps.
- Drop the basses out around A♭ Major.
- Continue until D–E Major. Encourage the young tenors to sing lightly through their upper passaggio.

Tips for Success:

- Even though this could be used as a descending exercise, it is more effective as an ascending exercise.
- Do not allow students to spread their mouth on the *Ee* vowel, especially in their upper range.
- Do not start the exercise too low. You will want students to sing in their head voices. Beginning in their chest voices runs the risk of them "pushing" their chest voices too high. If your younger treble voices are having a difficult time starting in head voice, start the exercise higher (F Major).
- Be very aware of all sections. If you are seeing or hearing tension, drop that section out as you continue to ascend the others.
- Modify vowels (*Ee* to *Ih*, and *Oh* to *Aw*) as you sing above B♭ Major.

 **Exercise 9**

Purpose: crescendo; dynamics; support

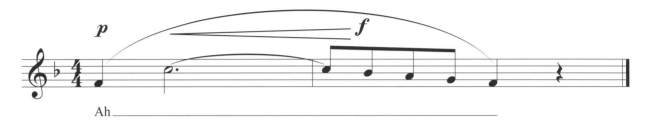

Ah _____

This exercise is great for introducing the *messa di voce* technique, which involves a crescendo and decrescendo on the same pitch. This is such an important technique for our students to learn. Of course, it takes years to develop and master!

This exercise explores the crescendo part of the technique. Make sure your students are not moving any part of the singing mechanism. They should keep their jaw dropped and still, their head level, and their tongue relaxed. A good image for them to visualize is that their air is the only "moving part" of this exercise.

6th Grade:

- Start in the key of F Major.
- Boys and girls sing in unison (above middle C).
- Ascend by ½ steps.
- Continue until around A–B♭ Major.

7th Grade:

- Start in the key of E Major.
- Ascend by ½ steps.
- Sopranos and altos sing in unison (above middle C); baritones sing an octave lower.
- Drop out the male altos as needed (or have them drop the octave).
- Continue until around A–B♭ Major.

8th Grade:

- Start in the key of E Major.
- Ascend by ½ steps.
- Drop the basses out around or before A♭ Major.
- Continue until around C Major.

Tips for Success:

- Start in a comfortable key, in which the girls and unchanged boys can start in their head voices.
- Make sure that the male changing voices are singing without tension in their upper ranges.
- Since this is not a range expanding exercise, be careful not to take the exercise too high.
- Be aware of their "moving parts" (jaw, head, and tongue) and watch for movement or tension.

 *Exercise 10*

Purpose: warm-up; vowel shape; diction; flexibility; placement

Zee   zeh   zah   zoh   zee   zeh   zah   zoh   zee   zeh zah   zoh   zoo

This exercise is a great one for focusing on vowel shapes and developing a forward focus. The "Z" will help put the sound in the mask. Encourage students to keep relaxed jaws as they sing the various vowel sounds. This exercise should be sung with great energy and lots of bounce at a pretty brisk tempo (♩ = 102). Give the *Zee* more energy than the rest of the syllables.

Find something physical (kinesthetic) for students to do to help them feel the pulse. Have them swing their arms back and forth, or have them shift their weight from foot to foot on each beat. You can have fun creating this bounce feel. Sometimes the best ideas come from the kids themselves.

After students get more comfortable with the exercise, replace the "Z" with "V" or "Th."

6th Grade:

- Start in the key of G Major.
- Boys and girls sing in unison (above middle C).
- Descend by ½ steps to around D Major.
- Ascend by ½ steps until around G Major.

7th Grade:

- Start in the key of G Major.
- Sopranos and altos sing in unison (above middle C); baritones sing an octave lower.
- Descend by ½ steps until around E Major.
- Ascend by ½ steps until around A♭ Major.

8th Grade:

- Start in the key of G Major.
- Sopranos and alto sing in unison, and tenors and basses sing in unison (an octave lower).
- Descend by ½ steps until around E♭ Major.
- Ascend by ½ steps until around G Major.

Tips for Success:

- Do not use as a range expansion exercise. Stay in the middle of their range.
- This exercise should be upbeat and have a nice bounce.
- Stay focused on their vowel shapes.
- Keep them from letting their "body involvement" get in the way of good vocal sound.

 ## Exercise 11

Purpose: strengthening the soft palate; diction; support

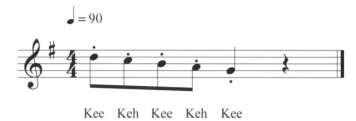

Kee Keh Kee Keh Kee

The main purpose of the next two exercises is to strengthen the soft palate. They also serve as warm-up and support exercises. When singing the "K" sound, the soft palate is automatically engaged. Singing with a raised soft palate creates a more open, resonant sound.

The staccato "K" should also engage the abdominal muscles. Getting the abs involved in the singing process will give students better breath support and a more intense vocal quality. Students should feel the "K" on the roof of their mouth and in their abs. Have them "slap" the roof of their mouth with the middle of their tongue, using their abs to "propel" the tongue.

6th Grade:

- Start in the key of G Major.
- Boys and girls sing in unison (above middle C).
- Descend by ½ steps to around C Major.

7th Grade:

- Start in the key of G Major.
- Sopranos and altos sing in unison (above middle C); baritones sing an octave lower.
- Descend by ½ steps.
- Baritones stop singing around E below middle C.
- Sopranos and altos continue descending by ½ steps.
- Baritones join again (in unison with the sopranos and altos) around Bb Major.
- Continue descending by ½ steps.
- Ladies stop singing around A Major.
- Men continue descending by ½ steps until around F Major.

8th Grade:

- Start in the key of G Major.
- Sopranos and altos sing in unison, and tenors and basses sing in unison (an octave lower).
- Descend by ½ steps.
- Tenors drop out around E♭ Major.
- Sopranos, altos, and basses continue descending until around C Major.

Tips for Success:

- Start in a comfortable key that's not too high.
- Remind students to use the middle (not the back) of the tongue. They will lose crispness if using the back of the tongue, and won't engage the soft palate as fully.
- This is not a range expansion exercise, so stay in the middle of their range. Singing too high could cause vocal tension.
- Make sure all five pitches are sung staccato. Making the last note short will keep it from getting heavy and pulled down.
- Watch their abs and make sure they are working.
- Some students may have a tendency to involve more muscles than needed. Bouncing the shoulders or rib cage should be avoided.

Exercise 12

Purpose: strengthening the soft palate; diction; support; resonance; flexibility

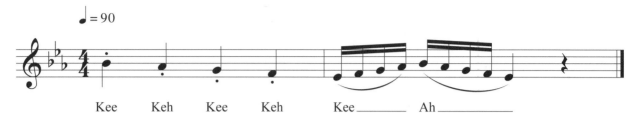

Kee   Keh   Kee   Keh   Kee_____ Ah_____

This is an extension of Exercise 11, and should be attempted only after the students are comfortable with the former. Before you add the second part, make sure your students have a minimum of body movement (except for the abdominal muscles) and jaw movement. The "K" will have helped raise the soft palate. The *Ee* and *Ah* vowels should have a nice space and resonant sound to them. Engaging the abs with the "K" will allow the students to sing clean sixteenth notes.

This exercise can be used as both a descending and ascending exercise. It is recommended that you start by descending. After you are sure your students are singing with minimum movement, start to ascend.

6th Grade:

- Start in the key of G Major.
- Boys and girls sing in unison (above middle C).
- Descend by ½ steps to around D Major.
- Ascend by ½ steps to around G Major.

7th Grade:

- Start in the key of G Major.
- Sopranos and altos sing in unison (above middle C); baritones sing an octave lower.
- Descend by ½ steps to around E Major.
- Ascend by ½ steps to around A Major.

8th Grade:

- Start in the key of G Major.
- Sopranos and altos sing in unison, and tenors and basses sing in unison (an octave lower).
- Descend by ½ steps to around E♭ Major.
- Ascend by ½ steps to around A♭ Major.

Tips for Success:

- Start in a comfortable key that's not too high.
- Remind students to use the middle (not the back) of the tongue. They will lose crispness if using the back of the tongue, and won't engage the soft palate as fully.
- This is not a range expansion exercise, so stay in the middle of their range. Singing too high could cause vocal tension.
- Watch their abs and make sure they are working.
- Some students may have a tendency to involve more muscles than needed. Bouncing the shoulders or rib cage should be avoided.

Exercise 13

Purpose: expanding the upper range; register transitions

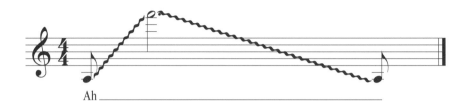

Ah

My students have nicknamed this as the "siren" exercise, because of the up and down imitation of a police car siren. The pitches notated above are approximations; each singer will have a different high note and low note. The basic idea is to have students begin on a low note and throw their voice up as high, and as quickly, as they can. They then slide slowly down to the bottom of their range.

The purpose of this exercise is twofold. First, it helps expand the upper range. It is a great tool for getting your young men into their high voices/falsetto. The main purpose, however, is to help with the singer's register transitions. The vowel *Ah* is used to help the singer maintain the open, "yawn" feel so they won't be tempted to tighten or close their throat through the passaggio areas. Most singers will be "sliding" through two register transition areas. Eventually, we want them to be able to do this without "cracking" or dropping an octave.

All Grades:

- Perform the exercise on one breath.
- Perform 2–3 at a time.

Tips for Success:

- When approaching a "break" on the way down, students should do three things:
    1. Slow down
    2. Open their throat (like the beginning of a yawn)
    3. "Push" more air through

- To get your students (especially the young men) to throw to a high enough note, try having them "throw" different things. The act of physically throwing something can help them get to a higher note. For example, have them throw an imaginary Frisbee as far as they can, and then follow its path to the ground with their voice. Or, you can have them pretend they are playing center field and are attempting to throw out a runner who is tagging-up on third base and running home.

- If they are having difficulty getting to their highest note quickly, explain that their voice is the reverse of a roller coaster on its first hill. The roller coaster climbs up very slowly with the steady "click-click-click," then falls down very quickly. Have them follow the path of a roller coaster as you "click" for them. Then have them reverse this and follow the path of a siren with their finger.

- The "Yawn-Sigh" is a similar exercise that can be difficult for your younger singers. Students begin on a high note in their upper range, and they "sigh" on Ah down through their passaggios. For many young singers, starting that high can cause tension. Many of them will "grab" the first note (glottal attack) and will proceed with a tight tone. Having them "throw" up to the high note keeps them from grabbing and allows them to sing with an open tone throughout.

 Exercise 14

Purpose: warm-up; developing the head voice

Oo

This is a good follow-up exercise to the siren. The siren allows your students to explore their upper ranges without worrying about singing specific pitches. This exercise allows them to focus on developing their head voice (unchanged boys and girls) and falsetto (changing and changed boys).

All students sing this in unison in the treble clef. The *Oo* vowel will allow them to achieve better blend, as well as a more forward focus in their sound. To help them develop a pure *Oo*, have them do the following four things:

1. Eyebrows up
2. Chin down
3. "Golf ball" in the mouth (imaginary, of course!)
4. Lips out

This will allow them to not only sing a pure vowel, but will help them sing with an active face. The exercise should be performed legato, without any bounce, with a little crescendo to the top note.

6th Grade:

- Start in the key of E Major.
- Boys and girls sing in unison (above middle C).
- Ascend by ½ steps.
- Stop around B♭–C Major.

7th Grade:

- Start in the key of E Major.
- All students sing in unison (above middle C).
- Ascend by ½ steps.
- Stop around B♭ Major.

8th Grade:

- Start in the key of E Major.
- All students sing in unison (above middle C).
- Ascend by ½ steps (basses drop out as they need to).
- Stop around B♭ Major.

Tips for Success:

- Make sure all students are singing the exercise in their head voice/falsetto.
- The starting note needs to be high enough to allow everyone to begin in their head voice/falsetto.
- Watch for the young men who want to lift their chin for the high notes. Encourage them to raise the back of the top of their heads instead. This will help elongate their spines.
- Use this as the 2nd exercise of a 3-part exercise (Exercises 13–15).

Exercise 15

Purpose: register transitions

Ah _____

This is a wonderful exercise to develop smooth register transitions. After Exercise 13 "opens up" students' upper range and Exercise 14 focuses on getting them singing in their head voice/falsetto, this exercise allows them to focus on eliminating their "breaks" while singing. They start in their head voice/falsetto and sing a descending major scale. Their ultimate goal is to make the register shift happen without a big (or eventually a noticeable) break. Singing on *Ah* allows them the feeling of a more open throat.

You will have many young men, whose voices are changing quickly, with a very pronounced break. In fact, when their voices break, they will probably drop an octave. This is perfectly normal, so let this happen. The alternative is to involve force, which means trying to "muscle" the note to keep it from dropping the octave. At this stage, we want the voice to do its own thing without manipulation, so the "missing octave" is ok for now. This also allows the men to sing with a more relaxed open tone. There will be plenty of time in high school to find the missing notes!

6th Grade:

- This exercise won't be used much until the second semester, when more of the boys' voices are starting to change and you start hearing "breaks" in their voices.
- Start in the key of C Major.
- Boys and girls sing in unison (above middle C).
- Descend by ½ steps.
- Stop around A♭ Major.

7th Grade:

- Start in the key of B or C Major.
- All students sing in unison (above middle C).
- Descend by ½ steps.
- Ladies stop singing around A♭ Major.
- Men continue descending until F Major.

8th Grade:

- Start in the key of B♭ or B Major.
- All students sing in unison (above middle C).
- Descend by ½ steps.
- Ladies stop singing around A♭ Major.
- Men continue descending until E Major.

Tips for Success:

- Make sure that all students are starting in their head voice/falsetto.
- Have them avoid glottal attacks at the start of the exercise. They should try to be as open and relaxed as possible.
- Sing at a comfortably slow tempo. Going too fast won't allow them to sing smoothly through their passaggio.
- Have students use their hands as a visual to help them. Both hands are held palm-up in front of them, with one hand higher than the other. The higher hand represents their head voice/falsetto, and the lower hand represents their chest/modal voice. As they descend vocally, they gradually move the higher hand down and the lower hand up. When they reach their register shift their hands should be on an equal plane. They then continue to raise their "chest voice" hand and lower their "head voice" hand. They are to look at whichever hand is higher through the entire exercise. Doing this will make them more aware of their passaggios and help them sing with less weight as they descend into their chest voice.

 # Exercise 16

Purpose: balanced onset; support; flexibility

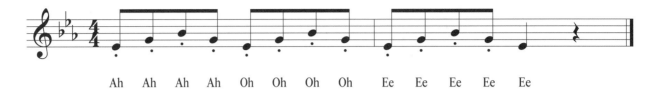

Ah Ah Ah Ah Oh Oh Oh Oh Ee Ee Ee Ee Ee

This is a beginning-level bounce exercise. Bounce exercises have a number of functions and purposes. They:

- Activate the abdominal muscles, which help develop better breath support.

- Develop vocal flexibility.

- Focus on the onset, or attack (beginning of the note).

- Help the singer develop a more intense, energized tone.

Each note should have the feeling, in the throat, of being sustained. The abdominal muscles stop and start the sound. In other words, the throat stays open while the abs do all the work. Avoid glottal attacks or aspirate ("H") attacks. This is difficult to hear in a large choir, so you really need to be aware! There should be minimal jaw or mouth movement.

This exercise can also function as a range expansion exercise, but make sure that you stop if you start to see tension.

6th Grade:

- Start in the key of E♭ Major.
- Boys and girls sing in unison (above middle C).
- Ascend by ½ steps.
- Stop around B♭ –C Major.

7th Grade:

- Start in the key of F Major.
- Sopranos and altos sing in unison (above middle C); baritones sing an octave lower.
- Ascend by ½ steps.
- All boys (altos and baritones) stop around A–B♭ Major.
- Girls continue until around C–D Major.

8th Grade:

- Start in the key of E Major.
- Sopranos and altos sing in unison, and tenors and basses sing in unison (an octave lower).
- Ascend by ½ steps.
- Basses stop singing around A Major.
- Tenors stop singing around C Major.
- Ladies continue until around D–F Major.

Tips for Success:

- If there are individual students who continue to sing with a glottal attack, have only those students put a little "H" at the beginning of each note. This will help them eliminate the "grabbing" feeling at the onset of each note.
- If there are individual students who continue to sing with too much air in their attack, have them think a little glottal attack for each note. This will help them get the feeling of a more intense attack. As they get better at the attack, make sure they ease off of the glottal attack to a more balanced onset.
- Help them avoid too many moving parts by making sure they aren't moving the jaw or mouth excessively while they sing.
- Do not go too high with this exercise until students have developed their upper range with other exercises. Without a solid foundation in their upper range, the potential for a tight, throaty sound is too great.
- Introduce the exercise at a slower tempo (such as ♩ = 104). Gradually increase the tempo to 140 or more, as they are able.

Exercise 17

Purpose: abdominal muscles; balanced onset; support; range expansion

This purpose of this bounce exercise is two-fold. One purpose is to develop the abdominal muscles. The other is to practice the balanced onset, or "imaginary H" attack. This balance between the strong abs and the open throat can help your young ladies get rid of some of the breathiness in their tone, in turn developing a more intense tone.

Perform it very slowly at first, then increase the tempo as students get better at it. Have students sing a tall, open *Ah* and connect it to the second note, which is staccato. Tell them they should feel the abs working like crazy, but the throat should stay open the entire time. If you hear them "grabbing" the first note of each pair, slow the exercise down until you hear balanced attacks consistently. You may need to demonstrate both attacks for them.

Be aware of the individuals who struggle with the "glottal" attack. Have them start each pair with a little "H." As they get more used to this, they can gradually get rid of the "H."

6th Grade:

- Start in the key of D Major.
- Boys and girls sing in the same octave (above middle C).
- Ascend by ½ steps.
- Early in the year, stop them around the key of B♭.
- Later in the year, continue until D–E Major.

7th Grade:

- Start in the key of F Major.
- Sopranos and altos sing in unison (above middle C); baritones sing an octave lower.
- Ascend by ½ steps.
- All boys drop out around B♭ Major.
- Girls continue until around E–F Major.

8th Grade:

- Start in the key of D Major, without the tenors.
- Ascend by ½ steps, bringing the tenors in around F Major.
- Drop the basses out around A Major.
- Drop the tenors out around D Major.
- Ladies continue until around F–G Major.

Tips for Success:

- Introduce the exercise at a moderate tempo (such as ♩ = 86). Gradually increase the tempo as the year progresses (up to ♩ = 160 with the older students).
- Build up to the high notes gradually through the year.
- Listen for balanced onset, and help students avoid glottal attacks or "H" attacks.
- Watch for excessive mouth or shoulder movement. There should only be movement in the abs.

 ## Exercise 18

Purpose: abdominal muscles; balanced onset; support; flexibility

Ah— Ah— Ah— Ah— Ah— Ah— Ah— Ah—   Ah

This is a more advanced bounce exercise, with the same two-fold purpose of Exercise 17. Tell students that they should feel their abs working like crazy, but that their throat should stay open the entire time. Perform it very slowly at first, then increase the tempo as students get better at it.

The addition of *re* and *fa* (Exercise 17 contains only *do*, *mi*, and *so*) makes this a much more difficult exercise, especially for your younger singers. Again, if you hear them "grabbing" the first note of each pair, slow the exercise down until you hear balanced attacks.

6th Grade:

- Start in the key of D Major.
- Boys and girls sing in the same octave (above middle C).
- Ascend by ½ steps.
- Early in the year, stop them around the key of A Major.
- Later in the year, continue until C Major.

7th Grade:

- Start in the key of F Major.
- Sopranos and altos sing in unison (above middle C); baritones sing an octave lower.
- Ascend by ½ steps.
- Drop all boys out around A Major.
- Girls continue until around C Major.

8th Grade:

- Start in the key of D Major, without the tenors.
- Ascend by ½ steps, bringing the tenors in around E Major.
- Drop the basses out around A Major.
- Drop the tenors out around C Major.
- Ladies continue until around D Major.

Tips for Success:

- Introduce the exercise at a very slow tempo ($\quarternote$ = 40) until all students are having success. Gradually increase the tempo (up to $\quarternote$ = 86, if possible) as the year progresses.
- Since this is a more difficult bounce exercise, do not use it for range expansion.
- Listen for balanced onset, and help students avoid glottal attacks or "H" attacks.
- Watch for excessive mouth or shoulder movement. There should only be movement in the abs.

Exercise 19

Purpose: diction/articulation

This is one of many diction/articulation exercises. The idea behind this type of exercise is to apply it to the diction concept on which you are working, and not to be overly concerned about tone, etc. Try many of these exercises with your choirs to find the ones to which they respond the best. Some work really well with younger choirs and not as well with the older choirs, and vice versa.

This is a great beginning diction exercise for the 6th graders. You'll notice that there are not many vowels to worry about (*Eh* and *Oh*) so they can focus on the consonants. Start the choir very slowly and gradually build up speed. Clarity is the goal, not just speed. As they get better and are able to go faster, you can have competitions between the different sections, or between the boys and girls. They love this! You will want to start this exercise with your 6th graders lower, probably in their chest voice. As they get more fluent with this exercise and with their head voice, move it up so that it's performed mostly in their head voice.

6th Grade:

- Start in the key of C Major (middle C).
- Boys and girls sing in unison.
- Start very slowly (such as ♩ = 50).
- Ascend by ½ steps.
- When you get to around F Major, start descending by ½ steps.
- Continue ascending and descending by ½ steps, speeding up until you stop.

7th Grade:

- Start in the key of G Major.
- Sopranos and altos sing in unison (above middle C); baritones sing an octave lower.
- Descend by ½ steps to around E Major.
- Ascend by ½ steps to around A Major.
- Continue ascending and descending by ½ steps, speeding up until you stop.

8th Grade:

- Start in the key of G Major.
- Sopranos and altos sing in unison, and tenors and basses sing in unison (an octave lower).
- Descend by ½ steps to around D Major (tenors drop out around E Major).
- Ascend by ½ steps to around A♭ Major (tenors join again around E Major).
- Continue ascending and descending by ½ steps, speeding up until you stop.

Tips for Success:

- Start at a comfortably slow tempo, gradually increasing as students become more successful.
- Make sure the focus is on diction/articulation (not so much on a beautiful tone).
- This is not a range expansion exercise. Singing too high or too low may cause tension in your young voices.
- Having your 6th graders sing the exercise in head voice too soon can make it thin with no power. For them to be most successful, let them get comfortable singing in their head voices before you have them sing this type of exercise up there. Once they are confident in their head voice, do these diction exercises primarily in that range.
- Hold a competition by having the girls sing it followed by the boys, or split it up into section vs. section. You will get their best, and they will have a blast!

 *Exercise 20*

Purpose: diction/articulation

Chest - er   Chee - tah   chewed   a   chunk   of   cheap   ched - dar   cheese.

Another of my students' favorite diction exercises is nicknamed "Chester Cheetah." It focuses on the consonant blend "Ch." Like with all diction exercises, the singers will need very active mouths. The "Ch" tends to make the front of their faces more active. We know that active mouths and active faces are a good thing in singing, and this exercise will reinforce that concept.

I think my students like this exercise because it's not too difficult to sing, and they can be successful fairly quickly. After they get pretty solid on it, try letting them change some words to make it a little more fun. (A recent popular substitution was "Justin Bieber chewed a chunk of cheap cheddar cheese." The students loved it – especially the girls, who would get emotional just saying his name!) The melodic pattern of this exercise can be used for a number of different diction exercises (such as "Mommy made me mash my M&M's, oh my!"), so once students learn it, they only have to focus on a different set of words.

6th Grade:

- Start in the key of C Major (middle C).
- Boys and girls sing in the same octave.
- Start slowly.
- Ascend by ½ steps.
- When you get to around F Major, start descending by ½ steps.
- Continue ascending and descending by ½ steps, speeding up until you stop.

7th Grade:

- Start in the key of G Major.
- Sopranos and altos sing in unison (above middle C); baritones sing an octave lower.
- Descend by ½ steps to around E Major.
- Ascend by ½ steps to around A Major.
- Continue ascending and descending by ½ steps, speeding up until you stop.

8th Grade:

- Start in the key of G Major.
- Sopranos and altos sing in unison, and tenors and basses sing in unison (an octave lower).
- Descend by ½ steps to around D Major (tenors drop out around E Major).
- Ascend by ½ steps to around A♭ Major (tenors join again around E Major).
- Continue ascending and descending by ½ steps, speeding up until you stop.

Tips for Success:

- Start at a comfortable tempo (such as ♩ = 100), gradually increasing as they become more successful.
- Focus on diction and articulation, and not as much on beautiful tone quality.
- This is not a range expansion exercise. Singing too high or too low may cause tension in your young voices.
- As in Exercise 19, have your 6th graders sing the exercise in their lower range until they are comfortable singing in their head voices.
- Focus on a strong "Ch" sound throughout the exercise.
- Don't let students get sloppy on "chunk of." They will have a tendency to sing "chunk-a" instead of "chunK oV."
- Hold a competition by having the girls sing it followed by the boys, or split it up into section vs. section. You will get their best, and they will have a blast!

 *Exercise 21*

Purpose: diction/articulation

A B C D E F G H I J K L M N O P   Q R S T U V Doub-le U X Y Z

This is another one of my students' favorite diction/articulation exercises. The Language Arts teachers like it too, as you'll see. It is fairly challenging at first, but they become good at it very quickly.

Once students get comfortable singing the exercise, add clapping on the vowels. (Watch out for "O," as it's the tricky one!) Then have them snap on the "Y" (the saying goes "A, E, I, O, U, and sometimes Y," thus the snap and not the clap like the others). Be sure to try this one first before you teach it to them!

When you add the clapping and snapping, go back to performing it very slowly, and then build up speed again. Your focus, again, is on an active mouth and a forward sound. Don't focus on the pure vowels, but don't let them sing ugly vowels either!

6th Grade:

- Start in the key of C Major (middle C).
- Boys and girls sing in the same octave.
- Start slowly.
- Ascend by ½ steps.
- When you get to around G Major, start descending by ½ steps.
- Continue ascending and descending by ½ steps, speeding up until you stop.

7th Grade:

- Start in the key of G Major.
- Sopranos and altos sing in unison (above middle C); baritones sing an octave lower.
- Descend by ½ steps to around E Major.
- Ascend by ½ steps to around A Major.
- Continue ascending and descending by ½ steps, speeding up until you stop.

8th Grade:

- Start in the key of G Major.

- Sopranos and altos sing in unison, and tenors and basses sing in unison (an octave lower).

- Descend by ½ steps to around D Major (tenors drop out around E Major).

- Ascend by ½ steps to around A♭ Major (tenors join again around E Major).

- Continue ascending and descending by ½ steps, speeding up until you stop.

Tips for Success:

- Start at a comfortable tempo (such as ♩ = 46), gradually increasing as they become more successful (♩ = 118).

- Focus on diction and articulation, and not as much on beautiful tone quality.

- This is not a range expansion exercise. Singing too high or too low may cause tension in your young voices.

- As in Exercise 19, have your 6th graders sing the exercise in their lower range until they are comfortable singing in their head voices.

- Hold a competition by having the girls sing it followed by the boys, or split it up into section vs. section. You will get their best, and they will have a blast!

 *Exercise 22*

Purpose: diction/articulation; dynamics; vowel shapes

My younger students love this diction exercise. Sometimes the 8th graders get too "grown-up" to sing it, and sometimes they will ask for it towards the end of the year if they haven't sung it at all. (They can get pretty sentimental!)

In addition to focusing on consonants, this exercise layers in dynamics and vowel shapes. This will help students develop their ability to focus on more than one thing while they sing. There are only two vowels on which to focus: "Uh" and "Oo". (You want to avoid "sewper dewper!") Focusing on the dynamic levels and changes in this exercise can help students when they transfer these skills into their literature.

If you want to make it a little more fun and interesting, try clapping on the rests following each "gum." So they would sing:

> Double bubble gum *(clap clap)*
>
> super duper double bubble gum *(clap clap)*
>
> super duper double bubble super duper double bubble
>
> super duper double bubble gum *(clap)*

Play chords on the rests for students to clap with.

6th Grade:

- Start in the key of D Major (above middle C).
- Boys and girls sing in the same octave.
- Start slowly.
- Ascend by ½ steps.
- Gradually increase the tempo.
- Stop when you get to around G Major.

7th Grade:

- Start in the key of G Major.
- Sopranos and altos sing in unison (above middle C); baritones sing an octave lower.
- Descend by ½ steps to around E Major.
- Ascend by ½ steps to around G Major.
- Gradually increase the tempo.

8th Grade:

- Start in the key of G Major.
- Sopranos and altos sing in unison, and tenors and basses sing in unison (an octave lower).
- Descend by ½ steps to around E Major.
- Ascend by ½ steps to around G Major.
- Gradually increase the tempo.

Tips for Success:

- Start at a comfortable tempo (such as ♩ = 68), gradually increasing it as they become more successful (♩ = 120).
- Focus on diction and articulation, as well as dynamics and the "Uh" and "Oo" vowels.
- This is not a range expansion exercise. Singing too high or too low may cause tension in your young voices.
- As in Exercise 19, have your 6th graders sing this in their lower range until they are comfortable singing in their head voices.
- Hold a competition by having the girls sing it followed by the boys, or split it up into section vs. section. You will get their best, and they will have a blast!

Exercise 23

Purpose: solfege; diction/articulation

This exercise breaks one of the main rules established in Section 2, but it is a fantastic exercise and well worth the exception. Since it has the range of an octave, finding the right key for your singers is imperative for success. You may need to start a little too low for your changing men in the 7th-8th grades, knowing that they will be able to sing all but a note or two. This will keep it from being too high for the rest of your singers.

The main purpose of this exercise is to get your students used to singing solfège. They may struggle at first, but they will be able to sing it faster and faster the better they get. Students absolutely love this exercise because it is so challenging to do well. And when they do it well, they take a lot of pride in their success!

6th Grade:

- Sing in any key from C–E Major, depending on the time of year (a higher key later in the year).

- Boys and girls sing in the same octave.

7th Grade:

- Sing in the key of E or E♭ Major, depending on whether enough of your young baritones have an E♭ .

- Sopranos and altos sing in unison (above middle C); baritones sing an octave lower.

8th Grade:

- Sing in the keys of D, E♭ , or E Major, depending on your tenors' low range and basses' upper range.

Tips for Success:

- Be aware of your men's voices! For the 7th grade, don't start the exercise too low for your young baritones. For the 8th grade, you need to consider your young tenors' low notes and your young basses' comfortable high notes.

- Begin at a comfortable tempo and increase gradually.

- For a challenge, have students sing the exercise as a round two beats apart.

- For a harder challenge, have the students use hand signs as they sing the solfège syllables. (This should be done at a slower tempo!)

 *Exercise 24*

Purpose: choral; intonation; tone quality

Chordal exercises are very important in the development of intonation, choral blend, and balance. There are countless different progressions and vowel combinations you could use. Find some that you like and arrange the voicing to fit your choir.

The basic I–IV–I–V–I chord progression is used in this exercise. This is written in an SATB voicing which, in this key, should fit your 8th grade choir very well. This key will also work for your 6th and 7th grade choirs. If you start in this key, this exercise should ascend by ½ steps on the repeats. You can use solfège syllables, one vowel shape, different vowels (*Ah, Eh, Ee, Oh, Oo*), or add voiced consonants (M, Z, V, Th).

6th Grade:

- Pick two of the upper three voices: either soprano/alto or alto/tenor (with tenor up the octave).
- Start in a comfortable key.
- Ascend by ½ steps for 4–5 reps.

7th Grade:

- Use the upper three voices; have the baritones sing the tenor part where written.
- Ascend by ½ steps for 4–6 reps.

8th Grade:

- Sing all four parts.
- Ascend by ½ steps for 4–6 reps.

Tips for Success:

- Start in a comfortable key for your young tenors and basses.
- Focus on matching vowels shapes.
- Focus on blend and intonation.
- Ascend as you repeat the exercise, so it stays in a comfortable range for all of the singers.

Exercise 25

Purpose: choral; intonation; tone quality

Soprano	Do Re Mi Fa Sol La Ti Do___
Alto	Do Re Mi Fa Sol La Ti Do Do Ti La Sol Fa Mi
Tenor	Do Re Mi Fa Sol La Ti Do Do Ti La___ Sol
Bass	Do Re Mi Fa Sol La Ti Do Do Ti La Sol Fa Mi Re Do

The last exercise is a favorite of mine. It is an intonation/choral singing exercise that really helps develop the ear, as well as sensitivity to the other sections.

This works best as a 4-part exercise. When teaching it, have singers use solfège syllables until they are comfortable with the pitches. Then have them sing on *Oo*, usually at a piano level. Repeat the exercise a few times, each time a little louder, and using more open vowels (*Oh, Ah*) as they sing louder. Have your choir sing legato, making sure they listen carefully to the other sections.

Besides developing excellent intonation, students are also reinforcing their scales. Many young choirs have difficulty with ascending *fa* and descending *ti* and *mi*. With a more advanced choir capable of greater range possibilities, move up a ½ step while holding the last chord, then start the exercise in the new key.

6th Grade:

- It is not recommended to sing this exercise, given its complexity and four parts.
- However, if your 6th grade choir is capable of singing 3-part music well, have students sing the upper three voices with your middle section (soprano 2) singing the tenor part an octave higher.
- Sing in the key of C or D Major.

7th Grade:

- Sing in the key of E♭ or E Major.
- Have the sopranos and altos sing their parts, and have the baritones sing the tenor part.

8th Grade:

- Start in the key of D or E♭ Major, depending on your tenors' low notes.
- Ascend by ½ steps to the key of F Major.
- Start *piano* and sing each repeat louder (optional).
- Start on an *Oo* vowel and open to *Oh* and *Ah* as you repeat (optional).

Tips for Success:

- Start in a comfortable key for your young men.
- If your young tenors and basses have limited ranges, repeat the exercise at the same pitch level instead of ascending by ½ steps.
- Teach the exercise using solfège syllables. After students are singing the scale well, switch to various vowels.
- The primary focus is on intonation. The secondary focus needs to be on matching vowel shapes and blend/balance.
- Be aware of your tenors in the low range, and your basses in the upper range. Watch for tension in both voice groups.

Section 5
What to Play As They Sing

NOTE: Recorded piano accompaniments are available for each grade's version of Exercises 3–12 and 14–22. They can be accessed online by using the digital code printed on the first page of this book. The accompaniments are provided NOT to allow you to get out of playing your own accompaniments, but to serve as models! In addition, using these recorded accompaniments allows you to roam through your choir as they warm up, identifying which students need additional help.

So what do we play during these exercises? We basically have three choices. The first is to play nothing, and that's ok sometimes. For example, I wouldn't play on Exercises 23, 24, or 25. Because of the nature of these exercises, what you might play could get in the way of what you are trying to accomplish. The second choice is to play chords in the left hand and play what they're singing in the right hand. The third choice is to play chords in the right hand and the root in the left hand.

Let's take a look at a couple of examples. We'll start with Exercise 6. The first accompaniment shows their vocal line in the right hand, and the chords in the left:

The second accompaniment shows the chords in the right hand and the root in the left:

The first accompaniment could be used until students are good at the exercise, and then you would play the second. The first gives them a good amount of support, both with the vocal line and the chords underneath. We replace the vocal part with chords on the second one. This still supports students and helps them develop vocal independence.

Here are two more progressions utilizing Exercise 7. This is a different exercise, but it uses the same basic idea. Once you get good at the second way of accompanying warm-ups (chords in the right hand), you'll notice that you can use the same pattern for lots of different warm-ups!

Next is an accompaniment for Exercise 9. This is obviously a more specific warm-up, but I wanted to share what I play on this one and why.

Students often struggle with the timing, especially when they are first learning it. They're not sure when to sing the second note, or how long to hold it, so I play what they sing to give them support. You'll notice that the C is played in octaves on beat two. This helps them find that pitch. If you tell them to listen for three chords after they hit the C, they will be more successful holding the note for its full value. If you crescendo during those three chords, they will be more successful with their crescendo. This allows them to focus on the skill they should be working on (*messa di voce* in this case), and prevents a non-vocal issue (rhythm) from getting in the way.

Even though recorded accompaniments have been provided as a part of this book, I would challenge you—using your own piano skill set—to develop your own accompaniments to your warm-ups. If you feel like your singers are really struggling with the melody, give them more support in the right hand. If they seem to be getting it, but are fighting what you're playing, stop playing their melody and play chords. Support them, but stay out of their way.

If you can't play I–IV–V chord progressions or scales in all keys, then start practicing! Do you know where the $200, 100-year-old upright that you bought in high school is right now? I do!

One final note on accompaniments: students will match the manner in which you accompany them. If you play wimpy, they will sing that way. If you pound and play unmusically, they will sing that way. If you play securely, they will sing that way. Middle schoolers are great at imitation, whether they are aware of it or not, so don't play like a wimp. Play strong, give them support, and you will hear great things!

Conclusion

I challenge you to become the expert on your students. When I started teaching 35 years ago, I realized my limitations. I cringe looking back and realizing how many there really were! I also remember how important those students were to me. When they walked into that classroom and gave me their all, I felt such a responsibility—a responsibility not to let them down as singers, musicians, or most importantly, young ladies and gentlemen. I knew I had a lot to learn about the changing voice, and the voice in general. I made a commitment to teach privately so I could learn from all of those individual voices over the years. I knew I had to become a better musician so I could challenge the best musician in my class. (Amber was the best musician in my classes during my first year of teaching. She sang beautifully, played piano for us when we needed it, and was a wonderful violinist. She was about the best artist I have ever seen at the high school level. Amber, thanks for pushing me to be my best so I could help you become your best.)

Many of us stop there. However, I think our biggest responsibility is to help these students become strong, confident, respectful young ladies and gentlemen. As teachers, we have such influence on our students. I don't agree with Charles Barkley when he said that he wasn't a role model. Every adult is a role model for young people. Our decision is what kind of role model we want to be. I think Charles may have been uncomfortable with the responsibility that comes with being a positive role model.

So again, I challenge you. Do everything you can to learn about the changing voice, male and female. Become a better musician, so that you can challenge your Ambers. Most importantly, be the best role model you can be, and challenge your students to be the best people they can be. My hope for you is that through challenging your students vocally and personally, you will look back on your profession with a feeling of satisfaction, knowing that you made a difference.

It seems appropriate to close with one of my favorite quotes. It follows my signature on all of my emails.

> *"Once you are interested in shaping children's lives,*
> *you will never be interested in anything else again.*
>
> *There is nothing greater!"*

Resources

Albrecht, Sally K., ed. *The Choral Warm-Up Collection: A Sourcebook of 167 Choral Warm-Ups Contributed by 51 Choral Directors*. Alfred Publishing Company, Copyright 2003, 21676.

Alderson, Richard. *Complete Handbook of Voice Training*. Prentice Hall, Copyright 1979, 0-13-161307-3.

Andreas, Esther and Fowells, Robert M. *The Voice of Singing: For All Concerned with the Voice—Singing, Teaching and Directing*. Carl Fischer Inc., Copyright 1970, O4823.

Crocker, Emily (edited by Day, Janet and Rann, Linda). *Voice Builders for Better Choirs: A Complete Resource for Choral Directors*. Hal Leonard Corporation, Copyright 2002, 08743260.

Crocker, Emily. *Warm Ups & Work Outs: For the Developing Choir*. Hal Leonard Corporation, Copyright 1989, 47123012.

Crocker, Emily. *Warm Ups & Work Outs: For the Developing Choir, Volume 2*. Hal Leonard Corporation, Copyright 1990, 47123027.

Dilworth, Rollo. *Choir Builders: Fundamental Vocal Techniques for Classroom and General Use*. Hal Leonard Corporation, Copyright 2006, 09970913.

Ehmann, Wilhelm and Haasemann. *Voice Building for Choirs*. Hinshaw Music, Copyright 1981, HMB-136.

Henderson, Laura Browning. *How to Train Singers*. Parker Publishing Company, Copyright 1979, 0-13-435511-3.

Jennings, Kenneth. *Sing Legato: A Collection of Original Studies in Vocal Production and Musicianship*. Neil A Kjos Music Co., Copyright 1982, V75.

Miller, Richard. *The Structure of Singing: System and Art in Vocal Technique*. Schirmer Books, Copyright 1986, 9780018726601.

Phillips, Kenneth. *Teaching Kids to Sing*. Schirmer Books, Copyright 1992, 0-02-871795-3.

Robinson, Russell and Althouse, Jay. *The Complete Choral Warm-Up Book: A Sourcebook for Choral Directors*. Alfred Publishing Company, Copyright 1995, 11653.

Walth, Gary. *Warm-Up!: 20 Purpose Driven Etudes to Develop Essential Choral Skills*. Hal Leonard Corporation, Copyright 2014, 00124188.

About the Author

Dan Andersen is in his thirty-fifth year of teaching. He is a graduate of Indiana University—Purdue University in Fort Wayne, where he studied voice with Dr. Joe Meyers and conducting with Mr. John Loessi. Mr. Andersen taught high school choir for eighteen years and is in his sixteenth year of teaching middle school choir at Center Grove Middle School Central in Greenwood, IN. At the high school level, his choirs were well-known throughout the Midwest, consistently receiving first division ratings at Concert Choir, Vocal Jazz, and Show Choir Contests. His middle school choirs have also received superior ratings at ISSMA competitions, as well as being featured three times at the IMEA State Convention.

He is a member of NAfME and a life member of the American Choral Directors Association (ACDA). Currently he serves as the Middle School Repertoire and Resource Chair for the Central Division ACDA. He is active as a clinician, festival conductor, and judge in Indiana, Ohio, Kentucky, and Illinois. He has served as guest conductor for the Indiana All-State Vocal Jazz Choir, Indiana All-State Middle School Honor Choir, and the Kentucky All-State Junior High Honor Choir. He was also the Vocal Jazz Ensemble director at the Indiana University Summer Music Clinic for 12 years.

Dan has also been involved in church music for over 35 years. He has served as choir director and director of music at numerous churches in northeast and central Indiana. He has also served as tenor soloist/section leader for several churches.

Dan is proud to have many former students who are actively involved in careers in music, many in education.